P9-DUU-272

To little adventurers everywhere

JANETTA OTTER-BARRY BOOKS

First published in Great Britain and in the USA in 2013
by Frances Lincoln Children's Books,
74-77 White Lion Street, London N1 9PF
www.franceslincoln.com

British Library Cataloguing in Publication Data available on request

ISBN 978-1-84780-318-4

Illustrated with acrylic

Set in Bokka-Solid

Printed in Dongguan, Guangdong, China by Toppan Leefung in March, 2013

1 3 5 7 9 8 6 4 2

Where's Lenny?

Ken Wilson-Max

F
FRANCES LINCOLN
CHILDREN'S BOOKS

There goes Lenny,
playing hide-and-seek.

Here's Daddy in the kitchen,
counting to ten.

Daddy counts.

1 2 3 4 5

First I caught a fish alive,

6 7 8 9 10

Then I let him go again!

Ready or not, here I come.

Where's Lenny?

Daddy hears a rumbling
in the cupboard.

"Aha!" he says.

But when he opens
the door nothing is inside.

Where's Lenny?

Daddy sniffs and follows his nose to the living room.

"Aha!" he says.

But it's only Mummy eating toast.

Where's Lenny?

Daddy sees something by the window.

"Aha!" he says.

But it's only Wilbur's wagging tail.

Where's Lenny?

Daddy hears
a bubbling noise,
but it's only
the goldfish.

Daddy sees some blobs of jam
and follows them up the stairs.

Where's Lenny?

Daddy hears tap, tap, tap
in the bathroom.

"Aha!" he says.

But it's only Mummy, fixing the light.

Where's Lenny?

Mummy and Daddy
rush into Lenny's room.

"Aha!" they say.
But no one is there.

Then they hear a giggle.

Mummy and Daddy creep towards the little giggly bump in the bed and...

"Aha!" says Daddy.

Here's Lenny!

Here are Mummy and Daddy
with Lenny, tickling
and tickling
and laughing.